Milly Molly®

B O O K S

This Milly Molly book belongs to

_____

For my grandchildren
Thomas, Harry, Ella and Madeleine.

Milly, Molly and Jimmy's Seeds

Copyright © Milly, Molly Books, 2001

Gill Pittar and Cris Morrell assert the moral right to
be recognised as the author and illustrator of this work.

Published by
Milly Molly Books
P O Box 539
Gisborne, New Zealand
email: books@millymolly.com

Printed by Rhythm Consolidated Berhad, Malaysia

ISBN: 1-877297-08-9

10   9   8   7   6   5   4   3   2   1

Milly, Molly
and
Jimmy's Seeds

"We may look different
but we feel the same."

One day Jimmy's desk was empty.

Jimmy wasn't the sort to stay in bed with
a cold or a bump. He wasn't the sort to stay
in bed at all. Jimmy loved school.
He loved being right in the middle of everything.

But best of all, Jimmy loved growing plants.
He always had something growing in a pot
or a packet of seeds in his pocket.

If Jimmy was sent out for chatting in math,

he always slipped off quietly to help the gardener.

But Jimmy never missed school.

It was very, very odd.

Jimmy's desk was empty again the next day...

...and the next.

When his desk was still empty at the end of the week, Milly and Molly and all Jimmy's friends were very worried indeed.

It was comforting when Miss Blythe
suggested Jimmy was probably sick with
the measles or mumps. Everyone expected
him to be back at his desk in no time.

Then one morning, Miss Blythe seemed different. She sat on the small chair in the middle of the classroom and asked everyone to gather closely around her.

She explained gently that Jimmy wouldn't be coming back to school. She said very softly that Jimmy had been taken to hospital and had died peacefully in the night.

Miss Blythe stretched her arms around
everyone and they all cried together.

Miss Blythe didn't mind that they missed maths or spelling.

And no one felt like singing or playing games at lunch-time.

Miss Blythe was happy just to chat and listen and give lots of hugs.

It upset Milly and Molly to look at Jimmy's
empty desk. But they didn't want Miss Blythe
to take it away either.

They decided to put a bunch of flowers
on Jimmy's desk and for a while that helped.
Everyone took part in bringing flowers from
their gardens and they kept Jimmy's bunch
of flowers fresh and beautiful.

When everyone was ready, Jimmy's desk
was taken away.

Milly and Molly very carefully put Jimmy's books and bits and pieces in a box for his mother to collect.

Tucked away in the corner of Jimmy's desk, Milly and Molly had found a packet of seeds amongst an extraordinary assortment of pens and pencils.

With Jimmy's mother's blessing, Milly and Molly
planted the seeds in the school garden on
a warm sunny day.

They watered and waited...
...and waited and watered.

On the twelfth day, a row of small green plants pushed their heads up through the soil. Every day they slowly grew bigger. Suddenly, the middle plant grew taller and taller.

It grew so tall it had to be tied to the fence.
And then miraculously, overnight...

...there stood a great big sunflower with a round happy face. Milly and Molly and all Jimmy's friends were delighted.
Jimmy was back again, right in the middle of everything.

Milly Molly

B O O K S

Other picture books in the Milly, Molly values series include:

www.millymolly.com